MARGRET & H. A. REY's

Catches a Train

Illustrated in the style of H. A. Rey by Martha Weston

WALKER BOOKS
AND SUBSIDIARIES

LONDON · BOSTON · SYDNEY · AUCKLAND

First published in Great Britain 2008 by Walker Books Ltd
87 Vauxhall Walk, London SE11 5HJ

2 4 6 8 10 9 7 5 3 1

This book has been typeset in Gill Sans MT Schoolbook.
Illustrated in the style of H.A.Rey by Martha Weston

Printed in China

British Library Cataloguing in Publication Data:
a catalogue record for this book is available from the British Library

ISBN: 978-1-4063-1406-9

www.walkerbooks.co.uk

This is George.

He was a good little monkey
and always very curious.

This morning George and the man with
the yellow hat were at the train station.

3

They were going on a trip to the country with their friend,

Mrs Needleman. But first they had to get tickets.

Inside the station everyone was in a hurry. People rushed to buy newspapers to read and treats to eat. Then they rushed to catch their trains.

But one little boy with a brand-new toy engine was not in a hurry.

Nor was the small crowd next to him. They were just standing in

one spot looking up. George looked up, too.

NEW CITY	6:30AM 8	OVERDALE	6:15 M 2
HILLTOP	7:00AM	LBURG	7:25 M 7
OVERDALE	7:15AM	CITY	7:50 M 6
SMALLBURG	7:45AM	G C	8:08 M 3
BIG CITY	8:00AM	TON	8:15 M 5
MIDDLETON	8:02A	WNSVILLE	8:40 M 2
OLD TOWN	8:45A	HILLTOP	9:25 M 1
TOWNSVILLE	9:10AM	OLD TOWN	9:55 M 8

A stationmaster was moving numbers and letters on a big board.

Soon the stationmaster was called away. But his job did not look

finished. George was curious. Could he help?

George climbed up in a flash.

Then, just like the stationmaster,
he picked a letter off the board and
put it in a different place.

8

ARRIVALS				DEPARTURES			
CITY	TIME		TRACK	CITY	TIME		TRACK
NEW CITY	6:30	AM	8	OVERDALE	6:15	AM	2
HILLTOP	7:00	AM	3	SMALLBURG	7:25	AM	7
OVERDALE	7:15	AM	4	NEW CITY	7:50	AM	6
SMALLBURG	7:45	AM		CITY	8:08	AM	3
BIG CITY	8:0	9 M		LETON	8:15	AM	5
MIDDLETON	8:02	AM	1	OWNSVILLE	8:40	AM	2
OLD TOWN	A:45	AM	2	HILLTOP	9:25	AM	1
TOWNSVILLE	9:10	AM	5	OLD TOWN	9:55	AM	8

Next he took the number 9 and put it near a 2.

George moved more letters and more numbers.

He was glad to be such a big help.

"Hey," yelled a man from below. "I can't tell when my train leaves!"

"What platform is my train on?" asked another man.

"What's that monkey doing up there?" demanded a woman. She did not sound happy.

NEWCITY	6:30	AM
HILLTOP	7:80	AM
OVERDALE	5:51	AM
SMALLBURG	:5	A7
BIG CITY	0:05	A
MIDDLETON	8:92	AM
OLDTOWN	A:45	MM
TOWNSVILLE	5:1	AM

The stationmaster did not sound happy either, "Come down from there right now!" he shouted at George.

Poor George. It's too easy for a monkey to get into trouble. But, luckily for George, it's also easy for a monkey to get out of trouble.

Just then the guard
shouted, "All aboard!"
A crowd of people rushed
towards the train. George
simply slid down a pole,

scurried over a suitcase and squeezed with the crowd through
the gate. There he found the perfect hiding place for a monkey.

The little boy with the toy engine also ran through the gate.

"Look, Daddy," he said, "a train!".

His father looked up. "Come back, son," he yelled. "That's not our train!"

15

But it was too late. The
gate locked behind him.

The boy began to cry.

George peeked out
of his hiding place.

16

He saw the boy's toy
roll towards the tracks.
The boy ran after it.

This time George knew he could help.
He leaped out of his hiding place and ran
fast. George grabbed the toy engine before
the little boy came too close to the tracks.

What a close call!

When the stationmaster opened the
gate, the boy's father ran to his son.
The boy was not crying now.
He was playing with his new friend.

"So, there you are," said the stationmaster when he

saw George. "You made a lot of trouble on the big board!"

"Please don't be upset with him," said the boy's father.

"He saved my son."

The people on the platform agreed.

They had seen what had happened,

and they clapped and cheered.

George was a hero!

Just then the man with the yellow hat arrived with Mrs Needleman.

"It's time to go, George," he said. "Here comes our train."

"This is our train, too," the father said. The little boy was excited.

"Can George ride with us?" he asked.

That sounded like a good idea
to everyone. So the stationmaster
asked the guard to find them
a special seat.

And he did.

Right at the front.

The end.